Reenie Gyse

✦

Katherine Starbird

Wekivacom

This is a work of fiction. All of the characters, organizations, and events portrayed in this work either are products of the author's imagination or are used fictionally.

For information regarding reprinting all or part of this book, please contact Katherine Starbird at www.katherinestarbird.com

ISBN: 0692372512
ISBN-13: 978-0692372517

To my parents
Who provided the wellspring of childhood experience
from which this story flows.

Acknowledgements

Heartfelt thanks to my husband, Chris, who gave me the time and place to write this story. Your faith supports me in all I do.

My critique partner Bettie Nebergall helped hone this story from its inception. Thank you Bettie for your friendship, encouragement, and wisdom.

Reenie Gyse

Chapter One

Elof had no idea he was trapped. The melody had coiled itself in the periphery of his consciousness like the tentacles of an octopus pulling its prey close, its beak poised to strike. He barely noticed the tune planing in his mind as he leveled his father's old spyglass on a sparkling gap between the headlands to the East.

His thoughts were securely fixed on the hardships of the ocean crossing. He relished every harsh wind, every bitter cold morning, every wild pitch of the boat on the waves. The more he punished himself, the more clearly he could imagine his father sharing the same suffering.

The late-afternoon sun peeked out from behind clouds on the horizon and shone pink and gold on *Skidbladnir's* tanbark sails. Elof turned away before his perfect agony was spoiled by the beauty of the moment.

After a hundred or so miles following the shoreline south, he'd had enough of coastal sailing. He needed to restock his provisions, then he'd head offshore again to embrace the discomfort of the ocean.

He tucked the spyglass between the cockpit cushions and consulted the chart. If a bay hid behind that gap, chances were good that he'd find a marina there and a market. The sweet taste of fruit not-from-a-can already tickled at the edges of his tongue.

The melody in his mind played on, soothing his mood. He began humming the unfamiliar tune. As much as he loathed the comforts of shore life, one night at a marina wouldn't kill him. With the boat tied to a dock, he'd get a solid night's sleep. In the morning, he'd stock up on staples and fresh produce and be on his way. Elof released the jib sheet and pushed the tiller of his father's boat hard to leeward.

Skidbladnir responded to the tiller with a sharp change of tack. According to his father, the boat was made of wood from the World Tree. His father had been a wellspring of boastful stories. He shared them with Elof to justify abandoning his family for months and years on end. What could compare to sailing on a magic boat, exploring the world, and imparting wisdom to the masses?

When he was a child, Elof had resented the boat for taking his father away. Now that he'd sailed her, he'd come to realize the boat was something special. Certainly not mythical as his father claimed, but she handled better than any boat he'd sailed before. *Skidbladnir* lithely dipped and skidded ahead of the wind, practically dancing across the waves as she flew up the bay.

As he approached the telltale forest of masts on the city's waterfront, a musical breeze whistled through the rigging of a hundred sailboats. The wind played an accompaniment to the tune in his mind. It sounded as though the clarion voice of a woman sang a duet with the breeze.

He allowed the tune to soak through him. He felt warm and relaxed for the first time in ages. Couldn't he enjoy a pleasant sail without begrudging his father the same experience? Pushing thoughts of the old man from his mind, he focused instead on the rhythm of the waves and the way

Skidbladnir's tiller tugged in his calloused hands. His uncle, the one who raised him while his father was away, would have wanted him to enjoy the journey for a change.

Elof filled his lungs with the salt air. Soothing lullaby strains rolled over him in time with his breathing. His head grew heavy. His chin nodded toward his chest.

The flapping of the jib brought him around.

The tune continued to play in his mind while he checked the set of the sails. The haunting vibrato could have come straight from one of his father's stories. He remembered believing there had been a time when monsters roamed the earth. The brave hearted fought flesh-and-blood dragons instead of shadowboxing their inner demons, the sport of modern man. Valhalla's golden walls rose in his mind, towering like a snow-capped mountain. An eagle circled high above.

The jib flapped again.

"What the…" He shook his head and the tune subsided. He'd never fallen asleep on watch before. Not in the light of day.

Looking up, he realized the boat was closing quickly on a breakwater of granite boulders that protected the harbor. Startled by how close he'd come to the rocks, Elof pushed the tiller away.

Skidbladnir's bow spun into the wind.

He lunged across the deck toward the main mast. If he could lower the sail quickly enough…

Skidbladnir bucked the oncoming waves, threatening to send him into the drink.

Gripping the handrail on the cabin top and then the stays, he worked his way to where the main halyard was cleated to the mast. Balanced with knees bent like springs and a hand on the rigging, he dropped the coil of rope on the deck.

The wind whipped the jib back and forth across the

foredeck and pushed the boat stern-first toward the boulders. They were close now. Very close.

He had to get the main down fast. "Come on girl," he said. "Don't fail me now."

When he released the halyard, the boat shuddered right down to her keel in protest.

To keep control of the halyard, he let it slip through his hands as the sail fell. If it went out too quickly, it would foul at the top of the mast and the sail would be caught halfway down.

He should have sailed away from the breakwater before he lowered the sail. He'd been caught off guard. He hadn't thought clearly. Gods help him, if he wrecked the *Skidbladnir* on a beautiful clear day like this, he'd never be able to face his uncle again.

"We're only taking a short break. I swear it'll be good for us both," he reassured the boat as he gathered up the flapping mainsail. Before the sail could catch the wind again, he lashed it to the boom. His blond curls whipped at his face stinging his eyes.

As he fastened the last tie-down, he pushed the tiller with his foot—all the way to port. *Skidbladnir* fell off the wind, her jib filled, and they cleared the rocks with a few feet to spare.

The weird tune stuck in his mind like a headache he couldn't shake loose. He was tired. He hadn't realized how tired, how desperately he needed a break, until he'd made that stupid mistake.

In the calm basin behind the breakwater, Elof lowered the jib. While he worked, he thought of something his uncle used to say: *A soft landing covers a multitude of sins*. The expression warned against rash decisions and crash landings alike. His thoughts were muddled. He should have been more careful approaching the harbor. He should have paid attention.

They were certainly moving cautiously now. Under the power of *Skidbladnir's* tiny mizzen, Elof sailed ever so slowly into the marina. He hummed the strange tune and fought to stay alert.

Chapter Two

An ancient-looking woman watched from the upper deck of a houseboat. Her lips moved in sync with the melody that lingered in his mind. Melody was too kind a term. It was more like a chant, dull and repetitive, an echo of the beautiful voice he had heard before. A creeping sensation ran down his back.

With only a small mizzen sail set, *Skidbladnir* was a different creature than she'd been on the ocean. Her heavy hull inched along like an elderly woman shuffling on arthritic hips. In fact, she wound through the maze of expensive boats so reluctantly he could have walked faster. *A soft landing...* Elof reminded himself.

They limped past the end of a long dock. There were no signs, but since it lacked mooring lines and dock boxes, he guessed it was the transient dock. If he were careful, he could squeeze *Skidbladnir* into an open space between a motor cruiser and a large sailboat. He'd only get one chance at this. Taking his uncle's advice about soft landings to heart, he tacked and lined up *Skidbladnir* to sail into the vacant spot.

A leathery old salt wearing only a faded Greek fisherman's cap and baggy trousers rushed down the dock toward him. "Probably wants to make sure we don't damage anything,"

Elof told the boat. Elof tossed him the stern line.

The man wrapped the line around a piling. Then he looked over the yawl and scowled. Elof followed his gaze to the white jerry jugs for fresh water that hung from the rail at the stern. A beat-up dinghy lay askew on the cabin top. Extra spars cluttered the deck.

Who was the old man to judge? A frayed rope held up his cut-off trousers. It was a wonder they hadn't fallen to his ankles when he reached for the line.

Elof hurried to tie off the bow. As he leaned over the side to wrap the line around the piling, a shadow swept over his head. The music in his mind abruptly disappeared leaving the arrhythmic clanking of halyards. *Strange*, he thought.

Something sharp raked across the back of his neck. The force of it knocked him toward the dock.

His balance gone, Elof grabbed for the post to keep from falling into the water.

Wings beat around his face. A furious caw sounded in his left ear. He felt the boat slide away from the piling.

His fingers dug at the tarred wood as he pulled *Skidbladnir* toward the dock. Only a lucky rock of the boat kept him from falling in.

The vicious wings receded.

Righting himself and gripping the line, Elof wiped blood from his neck, "What the hell was that?" he asked the beltless old salt.

"What was what?" a female voice answered. The woman from the houseboat stood with Beltless. A silver ponytail fell over one shoulder. A few wispy grey tendrils blew around her creased brown face giving her a wild look.

"That thing that attacked me. Something hit my neck." He held up his palm, streaked in blood, to prove it.

She looked around. "A seagull?"

"It hurt too fricking much to be a seagull. Maybe a

fishhawk." He searched the sky. There wasn't a bird in sight except for two pelicans cruising some distance away.

The man at the stern shrugged. "Can't say. Sure did scratch you up some. Maybe you caught the back of your neck on the piling when you went to wrap that line. Serves you right, showing off. What's wrong with using your engine?"

"Don't have one."

The man huffed. "You ought to get one, this being the 21st century and all."

"I made it here just fine without one. Is this a good spot?"

"Depends. You going to stay long?"

"Of course he's going to stay. Why wouldn't he?" the woman said. Her voice was by far the sweetest sound Elof had ever heard.

"I'm Reenie Gyse," she said extending her hand across the lifeline. Elof wiped his palm on his shorts. "Elof Gangrad. A pleasure."

"I said, are you staying long?" the beltless man asked again, drawing Elof's gaze from the woman's face.

Elof barely registered the question. Where he was headed? Why he had stopped? He felt a flutter of panic when he realized how confused he'd become. Then he remembered the fresh fruit, the empty hold, and the provisions he needed for the voyage.

"A night or two, I suppose," he answered. "Only long enough to restock. Is there a market nearby?"

Reenie Gyse's black eyes sparkled. "Just down the road. You can walk there and back in twenty minutes."

Beltless gave Elof a hard look. Reenie Gyse gave him an approving nod.

Beltless grumbled, "If you're going to stay overnight, check with the dockmaster before you get squared away." He pointed out an office on the far side of the yacht basin. "Most likely he'll make you move this tub." Without another word, he retreated to a small trawler on the opposite side of the dock and down several slips.

As soon as Beltless was gone, Elof stepped ashore. The masts, dock, and everything spun and swayed. He hoped it was only the effect of standing on a solid dock after being on the water. Reenie Gyse looked at him expectantly—kind of like the way a sparrow eyes a worm it's about to spear.

"Cheerful fellow," he said.

"O'Rourke? He's a sweetheart. All bluster, no bite." Her lilting voice was so melodious it gave his heart a flutter.

"Would you carry something over to the dockmaster's office for me?"

She asked so sweetly, how could he refuse?

Elof followed her down the dock. Despite her age, she practically skipped to her houseboat. As he walked, he noticed that where she stepped, she left a dark red smudge that could have been blood. Absentmindedly, he wiped wound on the back of his neck.

As she went, she sang to herself. What would he give to listen to that ethereal voice forever? He followed her down the dock like Alice chasing a vest-wearing, pocket-watch-grasping white rabbit. Reenie Gyse slipped through a sliding door on her houseboat just as Elof reached the boat. The closing door diminished the tune, leaving him feeling cut off.

A few moments later, she returned carrying a crisp ivory envelope. When she handed it to Elof, her fingertips brushed his palm. A tingle crawled up his arm.

The deep creases of her face smoothed into gentle wrinkles as Elof watched.

He blinked. There was no way he saw what he thought he saw. People don't un-age. Not like that.

"I was going to drop it in the mail to save myself the walk," she said as though nothing had happened. Proof positive, he was losing my mind.

The envelope was addressed to the dockmaster in an old-fashioned script that belonged on a wedding invitation. "Happy to help," Elof said as he folded and pocketed the envelope. He hoped his voice sounded normal. He felt quite dizzy.

As he walked down the dock, he kept to the center so he wouldn't teeter off. Between the spinning in his head and the arrhythmia in his chest, he wasn't feeling right. No need to panic, Elof told himself. The walk to the dockmaster's office would do him good. And if he keeled over here on land, someone would cart him off to a hospital.

Chapter Three

Reenie Gyse's tune played in his mind as he walked around the basin to the far side. His land legs hadn't entirely returned. He wobbled a bit going down the narrow extension to the office. He convinced himself that the dizziness and confusion came from spending weeks on the ocean in a little boat. It would soon pass.

From behind a counter strewn with charts, the dockmaster gave Elof the same hard appraisal that he'd received from Beltless O'Rourke. "Not looking too good, son," the man said staring over the rims of his reading glasses.

What a friendly group, Elof thought. "Was doing great 'til I got here." To loosen up the dockmaster's cold reception, Elof launched into the tale of his first ocean crossing. At first, he could hardly recall the journey. As he talked, the memories flooded back.

"One spell of rough weather, lasted over a week. The waves grew so big, they crested above the spreaders…" That was only a slight exaggeration, but he felt like he was becoming his father, telling tall tales. The old man filled his childhood with far-fetched stories of monsters, heroes, and gods from the northland. He also claimed Elof and he were descended from those gods. As a child, he'd figured out those stores were the product of an over-rich imagination, the boastful longings of an adventurer trying to justify why he'd abandoned his family to travel the world. Elof resolved to tell nothing but the truth.

"When I'd inherited my father's boat, my uncle put me up to sailing around the world. 'Wisdom comes from experience,' he said. 'And you won't get that sitting around home. You have the boat now—go, see the world.'" His uncle had also told him, "Since you resent your father so much, prove yourself better." He didn't share that part with the dockmaster.

"It's going well for you then?" the dockmaster said, shuffling through the papers on the countertop.

"So far, I've gone farther, faster than I sailed before, even with that storm. Might have helped, actually." Elof had conquered an ocean, which was a test, both mental and physical. And despite a close encounter with a whale and plenty of turtle sightings, he hadn't seen a single sea monster, not that they existed. They didn't. That was his point in making this journey—to prove the old man a liar.

Elof glanced at the charts. "It took a couple days after the wind died for the seas to settle down. That was the most uncomfortable part. That and eating chipped beef three meals a day after I dropped the can opener overboard."

"Never much had the desire to try that myself," the dockmaster said.

"The chipped beef or the sailing?"

"The offshore bit. Been comfortable here all my life. Though I did travel around some as a young man. Crossed the Gulf a couple times. That's about it."

The sun was low in the sky and Elof needed to get back or he'd be walking in the dark. Time, like everything else in his mind, had grown fuzzy. Remembering the letter, he said, "Oh, I have something for you." He put the envelope on counter.

"Mrs. Gyse. She's a piece of work, that one. Got all them

chaps sweet-talked into doing her favors. She didn't waste any time getting to you, either. Or did Barera put you up to bringing this 'round for her?"

"Just being helpful. Who's Barera?"

The dockmaster studied him for a moment. "You'll meet him sooner than you like. Go ahead and stay where you're at for now. Water and 'lectric hookup is extra." He thrust a contract toward Elof.

"Don't need the electric. Only water."

"Mark it on the form. Sure you aren't going to stay more than two nights? Got a weekly discount."

"I have to be on my way. I'm circumnavigating." The word came awkwardly, as though he didn't quite believe it. "I need to round the cape before it's winter down there or I'll have to wait for the next season."

"Hope I'm wrong, but I 'spect you'll be back, asking to stay longer. They all do, the one's that meet her right off."

"I'm not sure what that has to do with me. I'm not a coastal cruiser. Once I restock my provisions tomorrow, I'll be on my way."

"Listen up, kid. I'll give you one piece of advice. If the weather turns so as you think you ought to wait it out, get going anyway. 'Cause if you stay, you'll be stucker than stuck. You might never leave."

The man spoke so earnestly, Elof wondered if maybe there was mercury in the water supply. They were all mad, singing Reenie Gyse, beltless O"Rourke, and now the paranoid dockmaster.

As he left, the dockmaster called after him, "Do yourself a favor. Stay away from Barera and Reenie Gyse."

Elof didn't need the advice. In the morning he'd get his provisions and head out.

"Reenie Gyse. Reenie Gyse." The name played on his tongue and repeated in his mind like a catchy tune. Such a strange woman—ancient yet still beautiful, tiny and delicate but as lively as the terns that wheeled and dipped over the darkening water. No wonder the men in the marina were at her beck and call.

Chapter Four

The following morning, when he walked to the market for supplies, he bought too much to carry and had to pay for a cab ride back. He carted the groceries to the boat in a rusty shopping cart he found in the marina lounge. As he pushed the squeaky cart past Mrs. Gyse's houseboat, he saw her through the window. She sang as she frosted a cake with pale tangerine icing.

He was stowing the provisions when she called from the dock. She held up a frosted layer cake on a crystal cake stand. "My special calamondin cake."

"What's this for?"

"It's a welcome present. Bring back the plate when you're done."

"I'm only here for a couple days. No need to welcome me to the neighborhood." He accepted the gift anyway. It smelled deliciously sweet and citrusy.

Her black eyes sparkled merrily. "After you taste my cake, maybe you'll stay longer."

He couldn't help meeting her infectious grin with one of my own. "You know how to make a wanderer feel at home." When he had thanked her, he took the cake below to cut a piece. It filled the cabin with the fragrance of sour oranges and sugar and tasted like lemonade-in-a-cake and something else, a pungent citrus he'd never had before. One piece was not enough. He helped myself to another and sat down amid cans of beef stew and chili to enjoy it.

Through the open companionway hatch, he could hear Mrs. Gyse singing. A warm contentment spread over him as he contemplated how to repay her kindness. He cut yet another piece. He had intended to save most of it for later but couldn't stop eating. As the last forkful of cake touched his lips, a hearty voice called from the dock, "Hey yo!"

A broad-shouldered, short-necked man waited on the dock. His knife of a nose split a face round as a full moon.

"Reenie says she brought over a cake for you."

"Yes, sir."

"Figure you probably ate the whole thing. I came to collect back the plate before you forget."

Elof gave him the cake stand. "Tell her it was delicious."

"Tell her yourself. You know those calamondins are hard to come by. Would be good of you to search some out for her. She'd really appreciate that."

"I didn't catch your name."

"I didn't give it to you. It's Barera. And you are…?"

"I'm Elof Gangrad."

Barera nodded curtly and stalked away carrying the cake stand. He made a beeline for Mrs. Gyse houseboat. *They're really are all insane*, Elof thought.

He'd planned to leave that afternoon after stowing his purchases. The sweet cake made him groggy and warm, so he put his departure off until the morning and sat in the cockpit penning a few lines of poetry in honor of the citrus confection. He strolled to the lounge and posted it on the bulletin board with the for sale notices, inspirational quotes, and requests for crew members.

The orange ball of the sun dropped to the horizon. He picked up his guitar to pass the evening. Soon he found himself nodding off as he played. He put the instrument away and lay down on the quarter berth next to the companionway.

In place of his usual restful sleep, Elof dreamed he was imprisoned in glass. No matter how he struggled, he couldn't break free. The glass pressed on his chest so he could hardly breathe. He fought until he came awake.

The dream seemed so real, so urgent, that even awake, he struggled to inhale a full breath. He sat up in the dark and tried to get his bearings. His hands trembled as he lit the gimbaled oil lamp attached to the bulkhead. Once the globe was replaced, the tiny flame bathed the cabin with its warm glow. Pushing the curtain from the small window over the galley revealed the marina illuminated only by a few dock lights. All was still.

There was something about that cake. It had made him feel so good. Now his heart raced and his palms sweated. What had she put in it? He took a few slow breaths trying to expand his lungs and slow his heart. It was as though he was trapped in the paralysis of sleep, yet he was up and moving. When he turned his head, his equilibrium took a fraction of a second to catch up.

Not only that, but the sensation of being squeezed to death hadn't entirely faded. When he was a child, he had nightmares, so each evening as he went to bed, his uncle read him old Norse tales to fill his dreams.

He tried to recall the bedtime stories. Once he'd known them all by heart; now he couldn't remember their details. How could he have forgotten something that was so much a part of him?

Somewhere aboard along with *Birds of the World*, he had a

volume Norse tales that had belonged to his father. Urgently, he searched by lamplight. If he could only read the stories to fill in the blanks in his memory. *Curse Mrs. Gyse and her cake.* Not only was his body revolting, but his mind seemed to have gone too.

Tucked under cushions and in the top of the hanging locker, he found three partially filled spiral bound notebooks in which he wrote his poetry and song lyrics. It wasn't until he looked on the shelf with his father's spyglass and sextant that he found the leather-bound book tucked under the ship's log. He brushed the salt-stains from cover wishing he had treated it with a little more care.

Carefully he opened the book. Its pages were crisp with age and slightly warped from the dampness of the salt air. He turned page after page. Many of the stories seemed foreign to him. Some he'd forgotten entirely. Reading them as though for the first time was almost as unsettling as the trapped in glass dream. He'd lost part of himself. Thank the gods, he thought, that his father left the book onboard.

By the time the sky outside began to lighten, the volume had grown heavy in his hands. Too drowsy to snuff the lamp, he spread out on his bunk and laid the book over his face to shield the light. He drifted to sleep dreaming of Loki and of the dwarfs who crafted *Skidbladnir*, and what it felt like to sail across an ocean in a wooden boat.

Chapter Five

A sharp wind whistled through the rigging, waking Elof. The sky had lightened to a steel grey that made it hard to tell the time of day. He had the feeling it was well past the hour for the early departure he'd intended.

His head throbbed from the sweet cake and lack of sleep. He shouldn't have stopped here. Now with the poor weather, he could lose another day. Or he could brave the weather and just go. Outside, a curtain of rain moved across the water toward him.

Damn. If he waited for it to pass, he'd get too late a start. He brewed coffee on the alcohol stove, stowed the book and his guitar, and washed the plate and fork he'd used the night before. Everything needed to be ship-shape before he cast off. If he cast off.

A melody mingled with the raindrops drumming on the deck. Through his window, he could see Mrs. Gyse on top of her houseboat singing and dancing in the rain. Her yellow slicker whipped in the wind. She seemed delighted.

A gust shoved *Skidbladnir* sideways from the dock. Her mooring lines groaned a discordant note as they stretched. He really needed to get going, but the sudden gusts made it dangerous to leave the marina much less navigate the narrow pass at the mouth of the bay. He sipped the coffee and waited.

By the time the rain let up, it was too late in the day to set out. He'd made good time on the voyage so far. A few days weathered in would kill him.

The sky remained an eerie shade of steel gray. Elof donned a rain jacket in case the weather worsened again. He walked around the harbor to the dockmaster's office.

The man wagged his head and said, "Told you you'd stay, didn't I? You should cast off right now and head south like you planned, young man. There's nothing here for you. Nothing but rot. Quicksand and mire, that's what's got you here. You'll end up just like the others, not remembering nothing 'bout what they was up to before they came here."

Elof pulled out his wallet. "I'll pay for the two days I've been here plus the rest of the week for the discount in case the weather doesn't break."

The dockmaster took his money. "Quicksand, I say. You're as stuck as if you were up to your waist in it."

Whatever the dockmaster was on about, he didn't understand. He'd be off in the morning unless the wind kept up. Considering how quickly he'd made the crossing, he could wait a week or two and still cross the Southern Ocean in season.

Too restless to return to his boat, he walked along the wet sidewalks to the market in search of calamondins as a gift for Mrs. Gyse. If he found them, he'd be able to settle all his debts before he left. The little orange citrus wasn't easy to find. He ended up asking permission to pick some from a tree growing in a side yard almost a mile from the marina.

"Nobody eats those," the homeowner informed him. "They're too sour and full of seeds. Besides, they have an off flavor." Nevertheless, he gave Elof a used orange sack to fill and refused Elof's offer to pay.

"Glad to have you take them," he said. "They when they fall and rot, they smell god-awful. I've been thinking about taking down that tree for years."

Elof delivered the sack of fresh-picked fruit to Mrs. Gyse. She and Barera were playing cards in her main saloon. As soon as he recognized Barera, he wished he hadn't come.

"What a nice young man," Mrs. Gyse exclaimed, taking the bag. "Eddie, see what the boy brought me."

Barera looked up from his cards and nodded.

"Care to join us?" she asked.

Barera, the old tom cat, scowled.

"Thanks anyway Mrs. Gyse. Just wanted you to have those as a thank-you for that cake you baked."

"You enjoyed it?"

"It was delicious. Guess you knew that when Barera brought the plate back."

She hummed in delight. Her eyes glinted merrily. Elof felt the contentment that comes from making someone else happy, only with Mrs. Gyse, that good feeling was amplified.

She laid a hand on his arm. The tingling began immediately, spreading up his arm to his shoulder and down to his fingertips. Her hair glistened like freshly polished silver. She appeared much younger than he'd first thought.

Barera leaned back in his chair. A satisfied expression tweaked the corners of his mouth. Not a smile exactly, but he seemed wickedly pleased. He gave Elof the creeps. No doubt as soon as Elof left, the man would take credit for sending him for the fruit.

"I didn't mean to interrupt. I'll be going now." He left more abruptly than was polite. Mrs. Gyse protested that he should stay. Barera didn't look up again. He studied his cards and chuckled to himself.

❖❖❖

Back aboard *Skidbladnir,* Elof picked up the volume of Norse tales and tried to read. The stories seemed as cryptic as the dockmaster's rant about quicksand. He closed the book and put it back on the shelf with the sextant.

Around sundown, he brought his guitar out to the cockpit. This time he played some old songs his uncle had taught him. They reminded him of home.

Not long after, Mrs. Gyse appeared on the roof deck of her houseboat again. She executed some strange movements that might have been yoga or T'ai Chi. While she performed the slow intricate pattern, she sang. Her song cut through his, so he set the guitar aside.

After a while, he picked up his guitar again. When he began to strum, she sang louder. He played louder.

She turned, sweeping her arms up in a martial-art style punch aimed in his direction. Two strings on his guitar snapped at the same time.

He glared at her. *How had she done that? And why?* She had seemed so pleased with him when he'd brought the calamondins. Now she was like a force a nature, and angry force like the storms that swirled across the sky.

Things were definitely not normal around here. He recalled what the dockmaster said about leaving. He cast another angry look in her direction. This time, she was no longer interested in him. A calm determination had replaced the burst of anger. She focused on her strange dance steps. Her song wound its way into his mind. Where he had felt the sting of her rebuff, a calm sensation crept in. The stupor of eating too much turkey followed by pie had nothing on this feeling. It was all he could do to go below and crawl into the quarter berth. The thought flittered through his mind that now, while there was a lull in the storms, he should set sail. Before he could sit up, sleep overtook him.

Chapter Six

Another violent storm ushered in the following morning and the morning after that. He was weathered in. He swore at the sky, but there was nothing to be done for it. He'd have to wait it out.

Every day, he listened to Mrs. Gyse sing, mostly from the sun deck on the stern of her boat rather than the roof. Eventually, the weather cleared. By then, he'd become accustomed to the comforts of the marina—hot water showers, fresh food, and neighbors like O'Rourke and Mrs. Gyse. The vague recollection of a voyage played on his mind like memory that couldn't quite rise to the surface or a dream of future plans.

As time passed, he filled his days helping around the marina. On occasion, he'd sneak off to a nearby park to play his guitar and write his own songs or hide below deck to read his father's book. Mrs. Gyse seemed to not like those activities, so he did those less and less. Why get her upset over nothing?

One day he opened the book of Norse tales. They seemed strange to him, as though he'd never heard the stories before. He knew he had. He couldn't remember what his father looked like, either, only the animosity he felt toward him. His beloved uncle's face wasn't any clearer.

He tried to draw a picture from memory. The result was crude. He tucked the sketch between the pages anyway. Maybe if he practiced....

At night, dreams of confinement filled what little sleep he got. The dreams told him he should get back on the sea, continue whatever it was that he'd been doing when he landed here. Was it some quest to prove he was worthy of his father's name?

That wasn't it.

A challenge from his uncle?

The details were murky. Mrs. Gyse's songs were stuck in his head. With them filling his mind, there wasn't much room for thought.

Elof spent a morning helping Beltless O'Rourke clean out the marina lounge. The building was built over the water halfway down the main dock. It housed restrooms with showers, a laundry, snack machines, and an air-conditioned break-room where people who rented slips could hang out to watch television or read. Stacks of boating magazines and shelves of well-worn paperback books tended to accumulate.

When he got back to the boat, Barera had left cash and a note tucked between *Skidbladnir's* cockpit cushions in expectation of a bottle of gin. The man was too good to run his own errands. Elof took off to the liquor store right away. If he didn't he was sure to hear about it.

He was on his way back when he noticed a thunderhead building over the waterfront. The wind freshened and shifted bringing with it the icy scent of rain. As he reached the marina, the first drops splattered on the sidewalk.

He rushed up the dock and into the lounge. Its keyed outer door served as a security gate for the docks beyond. The door slammed closed behind him just as the glass door on the far end of the building flew open, caught by a gust. A woman darted inside. A bolt of lightning struck behind her.

"That was close," Elof said to her. The woman was perfectly made up with tight jeans and an expensive looking leather jacket. She resembled the larger than life characters on the covers of the urban fantasy novels that littered the lounge. Whatever he'd desired in women up to that point completely vanished. Here was the new woman of his dreams.

Her eyes locked on the bag from the liquor store dangling from his hand. She gave him a look of disgust. "You're not helping," she grumbled.

"It's not mine. Doing a favor for a friend."

Static electricity jumped from her, singeing the hair on his arm. "You look young, but you're just like that toady, O'Rourke, who's always hanging around my mother. With all the young meat interested in us these days, why she chooses to fade away with you marina rats is beyond me."

Before he could figure out what she meant, she practically flew out the door he had come in. She bolted down the dock toward the street. Lightning and wind chased her as she fled.

Elof waited in the doorway until the rain passed. As it cleared, he saw Mrs. Gyse performing a T'ai Chi-esque shadowboxing routine on top of her houseboat. Black clouds swirled behind her. She'd forgotten her yellow slicker and apparently had no respect for the power of lightning.

Chapter Seven

Mrs. Gyse was uncharacteristically quiet that night. While others slept, Elof holed up in his dimly lit cabin listening to the rain drum on the deck. He wrote songs to pass the time. The lyrics he penned revealed parts of his heart that he could not remember in the light of day. On sheets of loose-leaf paper, he scribbled verses about love and suffering, entrapment and addiction, lost time, and faraway places. It seemed to him as he read over what he wrote and refined his ideas, that these feelings might illuminate who he had been before he had come here. Everything beyond the marina had become as distant and unreal as a fairy tale.

When he was too drowsy to continue, he leaned back on his bunk with pen in hand and dozed fitfully until the wick burned down to a nub and flickered out.

The next morning, the rain had stopped. Mrs. Gyse still didn't sing. Elof felt the absence.

He hid out in his cabin studying his book. He was convinced the stories in his father's book could help him figure out who he was and where he was going. One story in particular seemed to hold the key to his understanding or lack thereof. He read how Odin sacrificed his eye for a draught from the well of wisdom. But why? There had to be a compelling reason to rip out one's own eye—other than insanity. Was it greed for the wisdom he would get in return? Or was it something beyond trading one kind of sight for another. Did the sacrifice have a more altruistic purpose, a higher goal? Elof turned the pages back to find what drove Odin to the well in the first place.

"Boy, you in there?" a voice called from the dock.

Elof's tenuous grasp on understanding slipped away. "Go away, you old geezer!" he called.

There was little chance of that. Elof closed the book and hid it under a cushion.

O'Rourke stopped by at least once a day to grumble about one thing or another. This time he carried a six-pack by the plastic rings, the first can already opened in his hand. Elof invited him aboard by taking the cans and pulling one free for himself, leaving Beltless to clamber over the lifeline on his own.

They sat in the cockpit sipping from ice-cold cans as a band of clouds drifted over the sun. The surface of the water roiled with a school of mullet, and a flock of squawking gulls circled at the stern of a charter fishing boat across the basin. The man was hardly ever at a loss for words, but he seemed to be having a hard time getting started today.

Elof tried to think of the story he had been reading, but without the book in front of him, he could only recall the cost —a god's right eye. For what? A moment later, he forgot about the book and Odin's eye. He had the uncomfortable sensation that he'd been thinking of something important but couldn't remember what it was.

Eventually O'Rourke said, "Looks like Mrs. Gyse is going to go. Her daughter came yesterday and told her she would have to move to assisted living." O'Rourke studied the rim of the beer can, "It's a shame, really. I tried to explain how we all look after her, but that just seemed to cement her position."

"How's that?"

"The daughter figured we wouldn't have to look out for her if she didn't need looking out for in the first place."

The woman rushing away in the storm must have been Mrs. Gyse's daughter. Now that he thought about it, there had been a strong resemblance. He imagined her trying to convince Mrs. Gyse to leave her home. He felt a little sorry for both women. Mrs. Gyse might be fragile, but she was strong willed. She wouldn't go without a fight. "It's a bad situation all the way around," he said.

O'Rourke had a faraway look. "Yeah. I'm going to miss the old bat. She always treated me well."

O'Rourke might miss his friend more than he let on, but Elof was relieved. She muddled his thoughts too much. He couldn't tell O'Rourke that. He wouldn't understand. Instead, he said, "She's a good neighbor. Made me a cake when I first got here."

O'Rourke's eyebrows rose in surprise, "You don't say? Her calamondin cake?"

"Yep. It was good. Ate almost the whole thing for dinner."

"Humph." O'Rourke didn't say anything else for a moment. "We have to convince her daughter not to make her move. All of us. You can do your part too. We're going to make her life as easy as possible here. Better than in a home where she'd be just another old woman, come to live out her few remaining years."

"Would that be such a bad thing? I mean, you devote all your time to making sure she's safe and happy. If she goes, someone else can look after her and you can get on with your life."

O'Rourke lunged to his feet, "How can you say that? She'd the best thing that ever happened to this place."

"But can you remember your life before you met her?"

O'Rourke looked as though he would take a swing at him.

"Is it really better now?"

O'Rourke face went slack for a moment. "I, uh..." he shook his head. "Can't say as I remember. It doesn't matter. She's a wonderful woman, and I don't want to hear you say otherwise."

Elof searched for something he could say about Mrs. Gyse that would placate O'Rourke, "She certainly sings well."

"That she does," O'Rourke said as he climbed off the boat. "Don't you forget it."

Chapter Eight

Despite secretly hoping she'd go, Elof did his part to help Mrs. Gyse stay. He offered to shop for her when he walked into town. He would have done that much without being asked.

Ed Barera stopped him as he returned carrying the bag of groceries. "Good to see you pulling your weight around here, boy. When you drop those off, she's going to ask you to scrape the barnacles off the bottom of the houseboat. You can use my scuba tank if you want."

"You're kidding right? She needs to get that boat hauled and the bottom painted."

"Tell her you don't want to help, but you know she isn't going to spend a week or two in a boatyard. All it needs is a quick once over with a putty knife. We want her boat looking good when the daughter comes back around."

Arguing with Barera was pointless. As far as Elof was concerned, the only thing the men at the marina cared about was how to keep Mrs. Gyse with them. They all knew he would be the first to climb to a masthead to make repairs or dive under a boat to free a line caught in a prop. The more he did for them, the more they asked.

He stepped aboard Mrs. Gyse's houseboat with the sack of

groceries and knocked on the sliding door. It opened with a squeak. She took the bag from him and set it on the dinette table as he stepped into the air-conditioned comfort of the cabin.

"Here, I want you to have this." She handed him a tiny green book, leather bound with gold-edged pages.

The cover was well worn and soft in his hands. "Looks special." He tried to hand it back. She refused.

"You've always got your nose in that fairy-tale book of yours. I thought you might enjoy these poems. One of my sisters was quite a poet in her day."

"She wrote this? Don't you want to keep it?"

"I want you to have it." She patted his hand. "You like poetry. You'll appreciate it."

He couldn't be rude and refuse such a gift so he thanked her even though it kept him in her debt.

"By the way, I was hoping you could help me out with something."

It could have been the gift or her dulcet voice that caused him to lose his conviction. Before he thought about it, he said, "I hear you need the bottom of your boat cleaned. Barera said he'd lend me a tank." He regretted the words as he spoke them.

She beamed at him. "You are such a sweetheart. I don't know what I'd do without you."

As soon as he began scraping the barnacles and algae off the bottom of the houseboat, every fish in the yacht basin came for the free food. The water, murky before he began, swirled with debris. He couldn't see more than a few feet, but fish darted in and out around him. A four-foot barracuda glided within arm's reach. He startled when he saw it, then cursed. The fish swam lazily out of sight.

How had he been conned into doing this job? Had he lost his mind? Fish bumped his arms trying to beat each other to the feast. He kept scraping. His breath rasped through the regulator. When he exhaled, streams of bubbles floated along the hard chines of the hull to the surface. He scraped his knuckles on the barnacles. Too bad Barera didn't have gloves to lend.

He'd worked his way half way down one side when something large brushed against his leg. A shadow glided away in the cloudy gray-green water and disappeared. Was it a shark? He tried to calm his racing heart by taking deep, slow breaths.

If it were a shark, it wouldn't want anything to do with him, not with so many tasty little fish darting about. He went back to scraping. His arms already ached. His legs worked hard pumping the swim fins to keep him close to the hull. The job would have been a lot easier if she'd had the boat pulled out of the water first.

Something attacked his ear. He spun around, thinking of the shark, blocking his face with his arm. A silvery fish darted away. The back of his ear ached as if it had been shredded to pieces. When he touched it, he didn't feel anything missing.

He surfaced and called to Barera. "There's a mess of fish down here, eating up the stuff I'm scraping off." He pulled off the mask carefully avoiding the injured ear. "One just took a bite out of my ear."

Barera bent over the edge of the dock to look. "Sure enough. Got a little blood there. I'll get you a cloth."

Elof treaded water, resting. In a couple minutes, Barera dropped him a washcloth to press on the wound.

"Doesn't look bad. It's already stopped bleeding."

He examined the cloth. Barera was right—there wasn't much blood. Thank goodness. All he needed was to gush blood into this seafood stew, especially when a big shark might be lurking. He threw the cloth back onto the dock next to Barera who untangled a cast net by holding one part over his arm and shaking the hem free.

"Hey, I'm going to cast for fish while you're working. Stay close to the boat. Wouldn't want to catch you." He chuckled.

Working his way toward the bow, Elof scrapped the barnacles off with a putty knife then scrubbed the leftover algae, sending more clouds of green into the turbid water. Gradually, he made his way to the bow and back down the other side, often peering into the shadows beyond his arms' reach. He couldn't see his own feet. Occasionally he would hear the plunk of Barera's cast net. The weighted edge would fall to wrap over the milling fish.

Something thumped into his upper leg. It knocked him against the boat's hull. At first, he thought it was Barera's net, but he hadn't heard it hit the surface. He spun around to see a gray and white form, a long tapered body. The tail fin tapped him as it flicked by. No doubt about it—that was a shark.

In a panic, he swam for the ladder. The shark was longer than he was tall.

He couldn't get his feet on the steps with the swim fins on. Grabbing the top rung, he tucked his legs as close as he could and pulled off a fin.

He popped his head above the water.

"Did you see that shark?" he called to Barera.

"Nope. Just saw you practically leap out of the water."

"That thing was bigger than me."

"Probably looking for barnacle tidbits like all the other fish. How much you got left to do?"

Elof's hands shook as he pulled off the other flipper and tossed it onto the swim platform. "Couple feet. Maybe 10-15 minutes more."

"Sooner you get it finished, the sooner you can get out of there."

"I'm not staying in. Not with a shark making like it's going to eat me." Pulling up as fast as he could manage with the tank on his back, he landed with a thud on the dive platform.

"If it wanted to eat you, it would have."

Mrs. Gyse appeared above him with a glass of ice water and a sandwich. "Climb up here and take a break. I made you a snack."

When he stopped shaking, he couldn't have been hungrier. He ate sitting on the stern deck, the scuba gear beside him. Barera entertained Mrs. Gyse with his impression of Elof's flight from the shark.

"It hit me so hard it knocked me sideways."

Barera grew serious. "You need to finish the job."

"No way. If I were meant to swim underwater, I'd have gills." He didn't belong down there any more than that shark belonged walking around on land. If they each stayed where they belonged, there'd be no trouble.

As he finished the sandwich, Mrs. Gyse began singing about sharks and minnows. Surprisingly, his fear of getting back in the water faded away.

"Okay, boy. Time to finish the job."

Against the voice in his mind that screamed that he shouldn't do it, he donned the tank, fins, and mask and stepped back into the water. He hardly knew what he was doing, but he scraped and scrubbed furiously while his heart beat like thunder. This time he didn't dare look around.

When he finished and climbed up the ladder, Mrs. Gyse was still singing. She offered him a towel to dry his face and looked as pleased as could be. Barera took the gear and muttered something about a job done well. Elof had nothing to say to the man.

As he walked back to his boat, his legs trembled from exertion and the dock seemed to spin. Even a cold-water rinse from the hose on the dock didn't clear his mind. Why had he lowered himself back into that murky water? What had come over him?

He climbed aboard *Skidbladnir* and sat on the cabin top studying the glassy surface of the basin. Blue oil stains and threads of sea grass flushed out with the tide. As he stared into the water wondering whether he was sane, the huge dorsal and tail fins of a shark essed along the side of the boat. Looking down on the shark from the deck, he figured it must have been eight or nine feet long. He shuddered. He'd definitely been out of his mind to get back in the water with that creature. He had to get out of here. The place was eating his soul. Pretty soon, there would be nothing left of him but an empty shell obedient to Barera's commands and Mrs. Gyse's whims.

In the calm of the evening, he released *Skidbladnir's* mooring lines and raised the mizzen and the jib. He swing the tiller hard over and turned the boat in the confines of the marina. Once he rounded the breakwater, he'd be free.

A gust of wind came up and hit *Skidbladnir* on the nose. He tried tacking. Whatever direction he pointed, the wind seemed to shift to remain head on. Only when he fell so far off the wind that he was headed back toward the marina did the wind shift favorably to push the little boat along.

He had never experienced such a thing.

Once *Skidbladnir* gained some momentum, he spun her around to shoot toward the mouth of the basin.

Again the wind shifted as though refusing to fill the boat's sails. For several minutes, Elof kept the boat heading into the wind. At first the breeze had been fluky, but now it remained steady from the northeast. Out on the jetty, a man who looked like Barera watched.

Elof pushed the tiller, heading the boat off the wind. Unbelievably, the wind once again shifted. It just wasn't possible. Elof gave his arm a hard pinch to make sure he wasn't in the middle of a frustration dream.

Harmonizing with the wind, the dulcet sound of Mrs. Gyse's voice carried over the water. Could it be possible? Was she controlling the weather?

"What's the matter with you?" he hollered at her across the water. He tried to tack again, but it did no good. The wind continued to shift to prevent *Skidbladnir* from sailing out of the marina.

The more the wind fought him, the more determined Elof became to leave. Then something changed. *Skidbladnir* seemed to come to life. The wind swirled as though it were battling itself. He couldn't make enough headway to clear the jetty but he wasn't forced back either.

Mrs. Gyse's voice carried clearly across the water, twisting with the wind, filling his mind. She was angry and it showed. The dulcet tone became strident, overpowering. The wind once again picked up, pushing the little boat backward. Elof turned her around to prevent her from being driven stern first into a dock.

As *Skidbladnir* limped slowly back to her berth at the transient dock, Elof clenched his fist toward the figure on the jetty and at Mrs. Gyse, who sang from the roof of her boat. All the suspicions he'd had about Mrs. Gyse keeping him captive were confirmed. Anger boiled, and his head felt ready to split. He would find a way to leave.

The headache grew worse while he tied *Skidbladnir* to the dock. He went below to lie down. The music in his head was so strong he felt nauseated. When it receded, he feel into a deep sleep.

Chapter Nine

Elof awoke with a headache and no memory of the night before. He didn't remember going out for a drink, but it was the most likely explanation of the throbbing pain. Either that, or he'd fallen and struck his head. He recalled a large shark cruising next to the boat and made a point of staying out of the water.

He spent his days helping around the marina and writing poetry and music. Whenever he wrote something that touched his heart, he posted it on the bulletin board in the lounge. Others in the marina might relate to the ideas expressed in the songs and poems.

As time passed, blue-lined sheets yellowed alongside boat-for-sale ads and crew-wanted notices. Whenever he finished a song, he added it to the board, stacking the poems on top of each other so they didn't monopolize the entire board. Maybe no one else looked at them—he'd never seen anyone read them.

One morning he'd returned from pinning his latest work and was preparing his breakfast in the cockpit when O'Rourke sauntered down the dock toward *Skidbladnir*. His baggy shorts barely clung to his thin body and his shirt flapped open revealing a chest tanned as dark as his arms.

Here comes trouble, Elof thought.

O'Rourke tipped his cap and looked over the boat with as critical an eye as ever. Then he asked whether Elof ever intended to go on with his journey. "You spun a good tale about how you were going around the world like your father had done, only younger. How it was your legacy. Seemed to me you had something to prove."

He didn't recall telling O'Rourke of his journey. He barely recalled it himself. He hadn't thought of it since—he couldn't remember. He vaguely remembered trying to sail away one night, but couldn't recall why he'd come back. Since then, the idea of leaving had made him physically ill.

"Guess I just got busy here," Elof said with a shrug. Truth was, he was adrift. He no longer had a plan.

"You should know," O'Rourke went on as Elof separated the black seeds from the soft flesh of a papaya, "some of the live-aboards are placing bets on when this decrepit yawl of yours will finally sink to the bottom of the yacht basin."

O'Rourke's bluntness didn't bother him. He was used to it. It was true that the voyage seemed like something ephemeral, a shadow of another life, but the boat, she was solid—she would never sink. That much he was sure of. "I hope you took their bets."

"Nope. It's Reenie Gyse. She has a keen eye for housekeeping and a lifetime in boats. She says the laundry hanging on the lifelines, the rust-stains, and the grime all hide sound chinking and a fresh copper bottom. I just don't see it."

"Mrs. Gyse is right. This is the best of boats. In fact, she can become anything—a Viking warship, a yawl as you see," he gestured with the hand that held the filet knife he used to separate the papaya from its peel, "or a life boat if it's made of wood. No way is she going to sink." He wasn't sure where the boast had come from, but it sounded good. Really good.

Skidbladnir's seaworthiness was about the only thing he could declare with conviction.

O'Rourke actually snorted.

"I mean it. Hold on to your money." Elof could imagine how with her lilting voice she took their bets. Later, her arthritic hands would probably collect more than enough money to pay her slip rent for the next six months.

O'Rourke didn't answer.

"You already paid up, didn't you?" Elof popped a slice of the sweet fruit into his mouth.

"Lost $10 bucks last month. But it's worth the price to hear her laugh and tell me I should consider my bets more carefully."

"Suit yourself." He offered O'Rourke a piece of fruit, but the sailor turned and stalked away. That man had a bad case for Mrs. Gyse.

He had a point about the boat, thought. Algae had taken over her bottom since he was reluctant to get in the water to brush it off. And he hadn't done much to keep the decks clean either. It wouldn't hurt to tidy her up a little.

That afternoon, Elof bought two mangos from a farm stand and a new mop head. He also stopped to get a bag of ice from the ships store on the far side of the marina. Then he went by the dockmaster's office to check on his application for a permanent slip. Since he applied—it must have been weeks before—he'd not heard a word from the dockmaster. According to the sign on the door, the dockmaster was out on rounds. He was always out on rounds.

Just as well. Elof wasn't sure he wanted to stay. He hadn't completely forgiven Mrs. Gyse and Barera for the shark incident.

When he returned, he dropped the bag of melting ice into the cooler on the deck of Padrick O'Rourke's little trawler, the Reenie G. The old salt didn't have a refrigerator and relied on the ice chest to keep his beer cold.

Back on *Skidbladnir*, Elof swabbed the teak deck smearing the sooty city grime over the entire surface in giant swirls. Then he improved it greatly by dumping a few buckets of salt water on the deck followed by a quick rinse from the fresh-water hose. He abandoned the mop and bucket on the foredeck to dry.

O'Rourke came by later and handed Elof a cold beer. He leaned against a piling at the stern of *Skidbladnir* chatting as Elof hung his weekly washing on the lifelines to dry. "You know, the dryer in the lounge is fixed. I'd be happy to give you some quarters so you don't have to hang out your clothes."

The man couldn't afford to subsidize his laundry. "I like my clothes air-dried."

O'Rourke looked away. "It's just that the dockmaster doesn't like the laundry. If you want a permanent slip, it might help not to hang the stuff out. I wouldn't get in your business, but we're starting to like you around here. It would help your case if you could get this tub cleaned up a bit."

"I swabbed the deck."

O'Rourke glanced around. "So you did."

"It's a matter of time, moving up on the list, isn't it?"

O'Rourke studied him and leaned forward as though about to let him in on a secret. "There's more room for interpretation in the rules than you'd think. Let's say the dockmaster wants to spread out the live-aboards for the security of the marina, he could put you off 'til something opens up in a different section. Fair enough, right? But just when a slip your size comes available, he could decide that all the live-aboards should be near each other, to consolidate the dock clutter or whatnot. He makes the rules—he changes the rules." O'Rourke gave a shrug, "You could be in limbo a long, long time."

Chapter Ten

One morning, Elof awoke to crystalline sunlight flooding through the boat's narrow windows. He'd dreamed again, but this time he'd seen a mermaid seated on the granite breakwater, her long hair flowing like water. Around her lay sailors so enthralled they neither ate nor drank. They basked in the warmth of a song she sang from the little green book Mrs. Gyse had given him. She lived for those sailors. The dream was almost as spooky as his recurring nightmare of being trapping in glass.

Some verses he penned the evening before lay on the bunk beside him. He sat up, rubbing his face to clear the dream from his mind. He read the song he'd been working on and then the others he'd written but not posted. He'd completely filled all his notebooks and bought a new one since he'd been here. The poems held such melancholy thoughts, so foreign to the lazy marina, someone else could have written them while he slept.

He took the latest poems to the lounge to add them to the stack on the bulletin board.

All his poems were gone. The entire stack was missing leaving a blank spot on the board. He checked the trashcans in the lobby, but the pages were not there among the empty cans and snack wrappers. He felt the loss. Who could have taken them? Why? They weren't so awful they needed to be destroyed.

That night he wrote about the sense of loss. The next day, he posted the new song with extra pushpins on the top and bottom to be sure it didn't blow away. When he checked the following morning, it was gone. He wrote another, and pinned it on the other end of the board, using more tacks this time. It too disappeared. Someone was stealing his poetry. He asked around about the missing pages, but no one admitted to seeing or being a poetry thief. Elof went on writing but whatever he posted was always missing the following day. He took to writing out a copy before he posted his work.

To find the thief, he spent more time in the marina lounge surreptitiously guarding the bulletin board while he worked on his poetry or chatted with other boaters. Around noon one day, after he'd done some work for Barera, he lolled on the vinyl-upholstered sofa in the lounge reading a boating magazine. He heard Mrs. Gyse singing to herself as she walked by. The words were disturbingly familiar. She had put a melody to one of his missing poems. He got up and followed her down the dock.

The tune was so moving he didn't want to interrupt, but when she climbed aboard her houseboat, he called to her. "So, you like my lyrics?"

She glanced up at him, black eyes blinking in the sunshine, "You posted those ditties?"

They weren't ditties but he wasn't going to be sidetracked arguing that point. "They were for everyone to read. Why'd you take them down?"

"You wouldn't expect me to come up with a decent tune standing at the bulletin board, would you?" She put her hand on his wrist and looked him in the eye, "I have to thank you. I don't get new songs very often." She sighed. "Sometimes it seems like I have already sung every song ever written."

His heart softened. She must like his poems or she wouldn't use them for her songs. That didn't make up for stealing them. At least they weren't lost forever. Or were they? "Where are the sheets I posted?"

"Oh, I have them. Do you want them back?"

It was ridiculous to be annoyed with her. She was an old woman, small and frail. And she hadn't meant any harm. "Just keep them."

Her black eyes sparkled in the sunlight and her face seemed to glow with her happy smile. "I'll sing you another one," she said.

"I thought they were lost. You should have told me."

She invited him aboard and sat him in one of the big PVC-frame chairs on the aft deck. Then she slipped into the cabin leaving him there. He wondered what she was up to, why she seemed surprised that he was upset about the poems, and he resented that she made him wait.

When she returned, she brought refreshments and a stack of crinkled papers, some faded and water stained—his missing lyrics. He set the pages aside as she poured him a glass of lemonade.

She sang one of the songs she had worked out to fit his lyrics. It wasn't half-bad, listening to Mrs. Gyse sing while he sipped fresh lemonade. Her song soothed away his annoyance and the deeper concerns his poetry exposed. Relaxed, he listened to the tune, all but ignored angst-laden words, and let peacefulness wash over him. He could get used to this.

Later, aboard *Skidbladnir*, O'Rourke drank his beer and regaled Elof with stories he'd read in sailing magazines. Even though the sailor couldn't remember his own youthful exploits, Elof imagined there had been quite a few. Then O'Rourke grew serious. "I heard Mrs. Gyse took your songs."

"She didn't mean any harm."

"Good. Wouldn't want any hard feelings between you. Our sailing group is going out for a night sail. Thought you might like to join us."

Elof couldn't recall taking *Skidbladnir* out since he had first arrived, however long ago that had been. It was a sad fact that most of the live-aboards didn't sail very often. It was a bother to unhook the electric and water and stow all their belongings. To remedy that, a group in the marina made a point of going out once a week on one boat or another. "It's good for our souls," O'Rourke had explained. "Might do you some good, too."

"What time?"

"Around sunset—on the Shamrock."

The Shamrock was O'Rourke's twenty-three-foot day sailor. He'd heard it was a lively little boat, but he'd not been out on it. He considered the clouds building on the far side of the bay. "You think the weather will hold?"

"Prob'ly." O'Rourke shrugged.

"I'll be there."

He should rejoice—he was finally accepted as one of them. It felt wrong.

Chapter Eleven

Elof studied his chart of the bay and tried to envision the evening's sail. It had been so long since he'd been out, he had trouble picturing how such a simple outing would unfold, each point of sail, the landmarks, the weather and seas. Yet in imagining the sail, a restlessness awoke within him that was hard to describe. He needed to escape the marina and his new life and return to the sea. He grew anxious to get out on the water again even if it would be with Mrs. Gyse and her friends.

The wind vane of a self-steering mechanism on a neighboring sailboat flapped in the breeze as though it was in secret communication with the windsock above the ships store. Throughout the marina halyards clanked against aluminum masts. If the weather held, it would be a good evening for a sail. Mrs. Gyse started singing. For once, he wished she would stop. He wanted to dream of sailing, and he couldn't when her voice consumed his thoughts.

When Elof showed up at the Shamrock, O'Rourke, and Mrs. Gyse were already there fretting because the battery was dead. Ed Barera had gone to search for a working battery to borrow. O'Rourke bailed a pool of brown water that stood ankle-deep in the cockpit. Little brown leaves littered the deck

—they had probably collected in the scuppers and clogged them. Elof was dubious about the little boat's seaworthiness. She looked so delicate he imagined her going under at the first sizable wave they encountered.

Barera returned empty handed.

"We could go on the Reenie G," O'Rourke suggested half-heartedly, dumping another bailer-full of brown water over the side. They wanted a sail and Reenie G was not a sailboat. Mrs. Gyse clasped her hands together excitedly and said, "I know—why don't we go on Elof's boat?"

Barera agreed. "You don't mind, do you boy? It'll be a real treat for Reenie to sail on a classic yawl like yours."

O'Rourke looked dubious. "You know that boat doesn't have a motor."

Elof considered the wind. "It's no problem sailing out of here."

The sky was darkening as they passed the breakwater and headed across the bay as close to the wind as *Skidbladnir* with her gaff-rigged sails could manage.

Tiny Mrs. Gyse took a turn at the helm. *Skidbladnir* was such a well-balanced boat that she had no trouble. While she was at the helm, Elof kept the sails trimmed. He watched the constellations appear in the sky and the phosphorescent wake and listened to the others talk with the camaraderie of old friends. It made him long for his uncle and his father, whose memory seemed more real out here on the water than they had for a long time.

"It's an odd name—*Skidbladnir*," Barera said.

"Means the best of boats." Elof pulled the long-forgotten detail from his mind without effort. The boat seemed to respond to her name with a flutter of her jib.

"How did someone as young as you come by an old boat like this?" Barera asked.

"She's been in the family for a while. I inherited." In a rare moment of clarity, Elof remembered the day his uncle gave him the boat. He had told Elof that to earn his inheritance he must travel the world and come to know its people. "A man isn't measured by his talents, but by how he uses those he's been given." All Elof could think of was how his father had left him home to go sail on his precious boat. He returned with wild tales of his adventures only to leave him again in the care of his uncle. An uncle was not a father.

Earning an inheritance like that wasn't exactly what he had in mind for himself. He wouldn't have sailed except his uncle insisted that he take the voyage. "What better way to understand your father," he'd said. Elof decided that it was a good way to prove his father wrong.

He'd been overly optimistic. "Seems like I was someone else back then."

Barera shifted uncomfortably. "You're too young for misgivings, son."

Elof turned his attention back to the trim of the sails. He didn't want to talk any more on the subject. Thoughts of those days filled his mind for the first time in what seemed like forever. His uncle had been proud of him as he set off to fulfill his father's legacy. If his uncle could have seen the black thoughts that resided in his heart, he wouldn't have been so proud.

Soon O'Rourke and Barera were absorbed in figuring out how to convince Mrs. Gyse's daughter to let her stay on her boat. After several months of delays, it was still a pressing issue among the men in the marina. Barera was prepared to pay out of his own savings for a caregiver if it came to that. Mrs. Gyse seemed far more at ease after that revelation.

Elof's heart felt heavy. Now that he recalled the journey, he again suspected she had something to do with the delay. He wanted Mrs. Gyse to go so he would be free to return to his journey. Unfortunately, the men practically worshiped her.

Barera was willing to give up his life's savings for her. He would have to find another way to get free.

She sang an old folk song in some other language. As she sang, Elof pictured her as a young girl, singing in a clear youthful voice. The men were entranced. Whenever she stopped, they begged her to continue.

When they came about, Barera took the helm and Elof sat with Mrs. Gyse on the cabin top and watched the sails and the stars. Her silver ponytail ruffled with the breeze as she chattered about her family and her childhood. Mingled with the sound of water rushing past the hull and the sails stretching and creaking, her voice was all the sweeter. It relaxed him, but now he was aware that it was an illusion, an enchantment.

Earlier, he had wished her to stop singing. The thought hit him that if she were to stop, it would leave a well of bitterness in his heart made all the worse for having experienced such sweetness. The loss might suck the life right out of O'Rourke and Barera. She was like a siren, singing all the time. He'd heard that the sirens couldn't bear to be defied. They'd die if someone actually escaped their trance.

What of the people a siren called? What of O'Rourke, and Barera? They'd become so entwined in Mrs. Gyse's world, they'd never leave.

On the third leg, the one back into port, everyone was quiet. Even Mrs. Gyse seemed to have fallen under a spell. Elof held the wheel in his hand, savoring the feel of the cool smooth wood and the gentle pull of the boat as she skipped up and down the waves. He looked across the cabin top to sight his course along the handrail. The old familiar wanderlust returned. It was a different sort of enchantment—the call of the ocean. It was present in the balance of the wind against the sails and the hull against the water, the balance of the helm and the keel working together to drive *Skidbladnir* across the bay.

Mrs. Gyse glanced at him. She looked startled. The wind ruffled her hair. She turned and began to sing softly as though she were singing a lullaby just for him.

To block out her siren song, he focused on the gurgle of water rushing past the hull.

Chapter Twelve

That night when one by one the lights in the other boats went out, Elof sat outside in the dark straining to remember his life before coming to the marina. During the sail, he'd recalled parts of his past that he'd forgotten, but he was sure there was more. He ran his hands over the cover of the volume of Norse tales and tried to recount again the day his uncle had given him *Skidbladnir*. But his thoughts kept drifting to Mrs. Gyse. It had been in his mind for a while, the idea that she was something of a siren. Until tonight, he hadn't considered that she might actually be one.

The wind picked up and whistled through the rigging of a hundred sailboats each at its own pitch. It reminded him of the day he first came to the marina. He'd said he would only stop for a day or two. Look at him now. He'd been too cocky—so self-assured he hadn't seen the danger.

All he'd proven was that he wasn't worthy of anyone's legacy, let alone the boat bequeathed to him. "Sorry, girl." He patted the cockpit combing. "I've let us both down, haven't I?"

The wind changed direction and lightning flashed over the bay. Thunder rumbled through the yacht basin.

"Well, I promise you, I'll get us out of this."

The storm came up fast. Elof dropped the leather-bound book into the cabin and gathered up the cockpit cushions before they blew away. He tossed the last of the cushions into the cabin just as thunder crackled the air then crashed nearby. Lightning lit the entire waterfront in skeletal blue. Mrs. Gyse looked down on him from the upper deck of her houseboat. Her arms were outstretched in a strange storm-yoga lightning dance, and she sang like an opera singer over the wind. The lyrics were his, the words he wrote the first night he couldn't sleep for feeling trapped. He worried that she might get hit and called to her to go below.

A branch of electricity hit the masthead of an ocean catamaran across the basin and ricocheted to a neighboring motor yacht and a wooden piling. Another branch struck the antenna tower on top of the ship's store, shredding the windsock and sending sparks down like fireworks on the row of fishing six-packs next to the gas dock.

Elof jumped down the companionway, skipping all the steps. Seconds afterward, a series of pops and sparks sounded in a poor imitation of the thunder as a transformer exploded on the wharf. The waterfront went black. He couldn't see Mrs. Gyse. He hoped she had the sense to get out of the electrical storm.

The next few strikes were farther away. From the open hatchway, he watched the ominous clouds roll overhead. Soon an acrid odor came to him on the wind. Flames began to light the waterfront, blocking out the ships store altogether and hopping across the driveway to a row of fishing boats under the covered docks. They clawed their way toward the yacht club docks and its rows of expensive sailboats and motor yachts.

Throughout the marina, heads poked out of hatches to see what was going on. Some men shouted and ran while others called for help or doused their boats with water. Across the basin, a man who looked like the dockmaster stood with his hands on his head, watching it burn. Padrick O'Rourke ran alongside the basin toward the fire. Mrs. Gyse was on the dock, dancing like a madwoman. Someone else would have to keep an eye on her. He meant to deal with the fire.

He freed the dinghy from *Skidbladnir's* cabin top and dropped it into the water, stern first. He tossed in the oars and the plastic bucket. The little boat barely moved when he jumped down into it. It just bobbed slightly to compensate for the added weight. He shoved off, fumbled the oars into the oarlocks, and pulled with all his strength across the basin toward the fire. It seemed like he was rowing through quicksand—everything was taking too long.

After a few strokes, the heat of incinerating fiberglass kept him from pulling any closer. The bucket was of no use against such an inferno anyway. He would have to do something else.

He spun the dinghy and rested the oars on the transom. The flames were so intense he had to pull his t-shirt up to protect his face. The futility, the idiocy, of facing down the fire passed through his mind. But then without knowing why, he stood up in the little boat. The wind whipped the flames over his head and pushed him backward at the same time. A flurry of sparks drifted above him and landed on *Skidbladnir's* deck. They quickly went out, but it wouldn't be long before more followed.

Suddenly, there was an explosion. Before he could cover his face, something struck him in the eye. He swore oaths so intense they would have called a rain of fire down on the marina if it hadn't already been engulfed in flame.

When he put his hands to his face, he could feel a large splinter protruding from his eye socket. Pulling it out, the shard of glass about four inches long sliced his thumb as well. Blood ran down his cheek. The wound on his face hurt so fiercely he couldn't open that eye. The shard was hot and burned his hand.

It clattered to the bottom of the dinghy. He sank to the seat to his dip hand into the water and ease the burn. When his hand hit the water, the flames to that side flickered. He knew what he had to do.

Standing again, he reached his hands toward the fire. The heat seared his open palms. Then it felt as though his hands became flames themselves.

Slowly so as not to rock his boat, he lowered both hands toward the water. Amazingly, the flames followed his lead, diminishing as his hands dropped. Like a puppet-master controlling the strings of a marionette, his hands were linked to the flames.

He pressed the heat down toward the oily surface of the water. The flames receded, but they didn't go out. He crouched, then sank to the bottom of the boat where he could reach over the transom. His burning hands sizzled when he plunged them into the water, first the right, then the left.

Along the line of boats, the fire hissed and smoldered. As he held his hands under the surface, the fire suffocated.

Once he was sure the fire was extinguished, he lifted his hands to feel his burning eye socket. He had a pretty good idea that the eye was gone.

When he had launched the dinghy, he intended to shovel buckets of water onto the burning boats. That had been a foolhardy idea—if he had gotten close enough, exploding fuel tanks could have killed him if falling roof debris hadn't. The only explosion was the one that sent the shard into his face.

He'd been out of his mind to attempt it. In fact, he'd acted on instinct from when he tossed the bucket into the dinghy until he put out the fire burning in his hands by dipping them in the water. He'd probably inherited such bravado from his forefathers. He remembered the Norse tales. It was possible.

He squinted at his hands with his working eye. Although they felt thick and tender, they looked normal—no charring, no blisters. Embarrassed and confused, he glanced around to see if he had an audience. A figure that could have been Mrs. Gyse stood on the dock near *Skidbladnir's* stern. He couldn't focus well enough to tell for sure. Huge raindrops plunked into the water all around him.

It took several long minutes sitting in the cold rain before he found the strength to grasp the oars with his singed hands and pull back to *Skidbladnir*. As he rowed, the sky opened in a torrential downpour. Great billows of steam rose from the fizzling embers of the burned boats. The flashing lights of fire trucks and police cars illuminated the fog in blues, reds, and golds. Their sirens screamed over the storm. Elof was lost in thoughts of the Norse tales and his legacy.

He climbed aboard *Skidbladnir* pulling himself up with a grip on the stays that cut into his sore hands. Rainwater rolled into his face, blinding him as he pulled the dinghy aboard. His hands shook as he tied the lashings. His fingers were numb. All the while, his mind raced. He'd been living in a trance where confusion muddled his thoughts and distorted them until he hardly knew who he was. Now that he was thinking more clearly, one thought overrode all else—he had to get away before he was lost forever.

Chapter Thirteen

Mrs. Gyse called to him. She stood on the dock holding up a towel in the rain. The towel looked as wet as she was. "Wrap this around yourself young man. You'll catch the death of cold if you don't dry off."

"Thank you, Mrs. Gyse." She was the last person he wanted to see, but he took the towel because she offered it. "I'll be fine. You need to get out of the rain too."

She shivered in her robe with wet hair plastered to her head and the rain pelting all around. "Well that was some excitement, wasn't it?" Even though she had to yell to be heard, her voice was as sweet as ever.

Had she seen him calm the fire? "Good thing it started raining when it did," he said, "or the whole marina might have gone up in flames."

She'd given him the towel, why didn't she leave? Instead, she stared as though she'd never seen him before. He kept his right eye firmly closed and squinted at her through the other. "I'm going below; you should get back inside too."

She didn't move.

"Do you want me to walk you back to your boat?"

"Thor used to be the god of thunder," she muttered,

sounding dazed.

It was possible she wasn't right in the head. Or she was just a sweet elderly woman struggling with a touch of dementia while he was the crazy one for thinking her a siren. He imagined her confusedly walking off the edge of the dock and decided to help her home whether she wanted help or not. They walked toward her boat with his hand on her arm to steady her, just in case. "It was only a thunderstorm," he said.

"I know, I know." She pulled her arm away and faced him. "Now Odin, he could put out fires."

The recent lucidity came in waves. He felt disoriented. If he was going to break out of whatever held him in this state of confusion, he had to keep in mind who he really was. He was no Odin; that was for sure. But now that he had done what he had done with the flames, it was hard to deny that something of Odin's legacy lived in him.

"I'm not Odin, Mrs. Gyse. I don't know what happened. Believe me, I'm nothing like the old man."

She looked up at him with searching eyes and patted his hand. "Of course you're not. Why would you say such a silly thing? You are nothing like Odin. Odin was an old blind man with a staff and a blue cape and a boat he could fold up and carry away in his pocket."

"That would be a nice trick," he said politely. "While we're talking of the old tales, my uncle used to tell me of sirens who lured sailors to their death upon the rocks."

She hesitated, seeming surprised that he might recognize her. "Only figuratively," she said.

"Of course." The less he said, the sooner he could have her back at her boat.

"Wait here," she said when they arrived at her houseboat. "I have something I've been meaning to give you."

"I can't, Mrs. Gyse. I need to go."

"You wait. Won't take me but a second." Before he could

protest again, she ducked aboard and into the cabin, sliding the glass door closed behind her.

He hung the sodden towel on the railing at the stern. Waiting for her seemed wrong. It reminded him of the power she held. He had his wounds to tend. He couldn't wait any longer.

As he walked away, the shriek of the glass door sliding open made him turn back. She rushed back onto the dock carrying a cut-crystal bottle with thick orange-colored liqueur sloshing inside. "To warm you up," she said wistfully, offering it to him. "It's from calamondins you gave me when you first arrived. I made it for you."

"You've given me too much already." He took the gift anyway.

He studied the bottle in his hand. In the time it had taken to make that liqueur, months had slipped away. He tried to figure how long it had been since he first tied *Skidbladnir* to this dock. He couldn't remember the seasons. He sensed they had changed around him. The act of thinking about time's passage was like swimming for the surface after being under water too long. It had been long, far longer than he intended.

"Taste it."

"No, I'll keep it for later to remember you by."

He was suffocating, pressed in on all sides as though he were deep underwater. He had to fight to the surface. Frantically, he worked his befuddled mind.

Her song washed over his thoughts. The words she sang were his. They told of evils in the world and an absent hero. Like a child, he again felt the emptiness his father left when he was gone. How long ago was that?

His vision went dark. Hollowness grew from inside him until it encompassed the world. Within it, he saw four beasts. The first two, broad-backed Disillusionment and Hopelessness climbed together from the coldest reaches of Hel. Cruelty with spiked horns and razor-sharp teeth strode toward him from the South, reaping huge swaths of humanity and leaving them to rot where they fell. Flowing from the North, the creeping blight of Apathy spread like tar across the world blotting out all light. The beasts hemmed him in and pulled him down into a dark abyss.

Ceasing to struggle, he sank back into the flowing gentleness of Mrs. Gyse's melody.

His mind's eye drifted downward in turbid water. He watched as the beasts drew him deeper. His body came to rest on solid rock. His lungs burned.

The world deserved a future, one where children played and parents loved. Strangers performed acts of kindness and friends encouraged each other.

The vision of hope spurred him to fight toward the surface. Toward clarity. Toward freedom from her spell. Good and evil compressed as though time no longer existed. He saw all things at once.

The present expanded again with the air that filled his lungs.

It didn't matter whether months or seasons or years had passed, merely appreciating that the time had ebbed worked against the enchantment.

The sharp edges of the crystal cut into his palm as his fist clenched. He didn't want her gifts. Would she not stop that infernal singing that made it so hard to think clearly?

He threw the bottle at her feet and it shattered on the concrete dock. The orange liqueur bled with the rainwater releasing a sickie-sweet odor.

Her song became like a crow's caw. Her flowing hair, now wet and stringy, looked to him like the ruffled grey feathers of a dead gull.

"You've kept me here too long," he said. "I'm leaving."

She shifted uneasily, shards of crystal around her feet. "I

don't understand. You were not unhappy." It was almost a question.

She'd never let him go. She wouldn't understand how staying here felt like being weathered-in for eternity. He had a future.

What of the others? Could he leave them? He thought of Padrick O'Rourke who had been here for ages; Ed Barera who would give anything to make her happy; and her daughter, who was planning to move Mrs. Gyse away. "You will have to let them go too, O'Rourke and Barera and the others."

She looked at him with her inquisitive bird-like stare, "Why do you say that?"

"You aren't going to be here forever. What will happen to them when your daughter takes you away?"

"Haven't you heard? It's all arranged; Eddie Barera talked to her and I can stay."

"I could take them all with me," he said. She'd take it as the threat he intended.

Her eyes widened in panic. "Traitor," she shrieked. "You wouldn't."

"I will if you try to keep me here any longer." He couldn't take them, he knew. They would turn on him to protect her. If he did manage to carry them beyond her call, she would wither and die without their adoration. And they, their identities so intertwined in hers, might succumb to their grief. He already felt the hollowness of that grief himself. He wouldn't be the instrument that brought it on the others.

She didn't know that. She believed his threat. As long as she feared what he might do, he had hope.

"I am going," he said with renewed conviction.

"Go then," she cawed. "No one here will stop you." All the beauty was gone from her voice and he felt sadder still. Despite all her tricks and conniving, he cared for her. It was as though a part of him died as another part was reborn.

Much later, when the rain stopped and the wind died, the power company trucks had gone and the neighbors had returned to sleep, Elof slipped out of his cabin and onto the dock. He'd fashioned a bandage for his eye. His hands were sore from the fire, but he felt stronger than he had in ages. The marina was still and soundless. The halyards didn't clank and the boats didn't rock. Even the mullet seemed to be asleep. He looked around and saw that from the window of her houseboat, Mrs. Gyse watched. Her lips moved as though she was singing; he couldn't hear her.

Despite the intense stillness, he was sure *Skidbladnir* could have sailed out of the marina, across the bay, and out into the open ocean. Because Mrs. Gyse watched, he stepped lightly onto the dock and released the mooring lines. He took one of the spars from the deck and dropped it onto the dock.

Then holding *Skidbladnir* by the bowsprit, he twisted and folded the boat into halves and quarters and triangles. With the first twist, the rigging tucked in like a child's pop-up book closing. With each fold, *Skidbladnir* became smaller and lighter until the boat was reduced to a little packet that fit neatly into his pocket.

With an impish smile in her direction, he picked up the spar-turned-walking-stick and strode past her out of the marina just as his father the wanderer would have done. He'd catch a ride down the coast and continue his journey.

About the Author

Katherine Starbird is a fiction writer whose rich prose brings fantastical elements into the familiar world. Her wildly inventive stories are populated by vivid characters such as an orphaned young heir to Odin, a siren in a city marina, and a shape-shifting goddess masquerading as an ordinary human in modern Washington, DC. No matter how outlandish or out of place her characters are, their epic-sized desires create problems to which readers relate in a very human and endearing way. Her debut novel, *The Jaguar Key*, received a Royal Palm Literary Award from the Florida Writers Association.

Katherine Starbird is originally from St. Petersburg, Florida. She spent much of her childhood on or around the water—collecting shells or hunting sea critters in the flats near her home. Her parents, both teachers, were avid sailors and took the family on cruises during the summer months. Sailing introduced her to new and interesting places that she draws upon in her stories. In college, she studied psychology and religion, subjects that serve her well as an author.

She currently lives in Central Florida with her husband and children. She enjoys traveling and exploring the outdoors with her family.

To learn more about Katherine Starbird and her current projects, check her website: www.katherinestarbird.com. There you will find links to purchase her other books as well.